INSTRUMENTAL PLAY-ALONG

MOVIE HITS

Trumpet

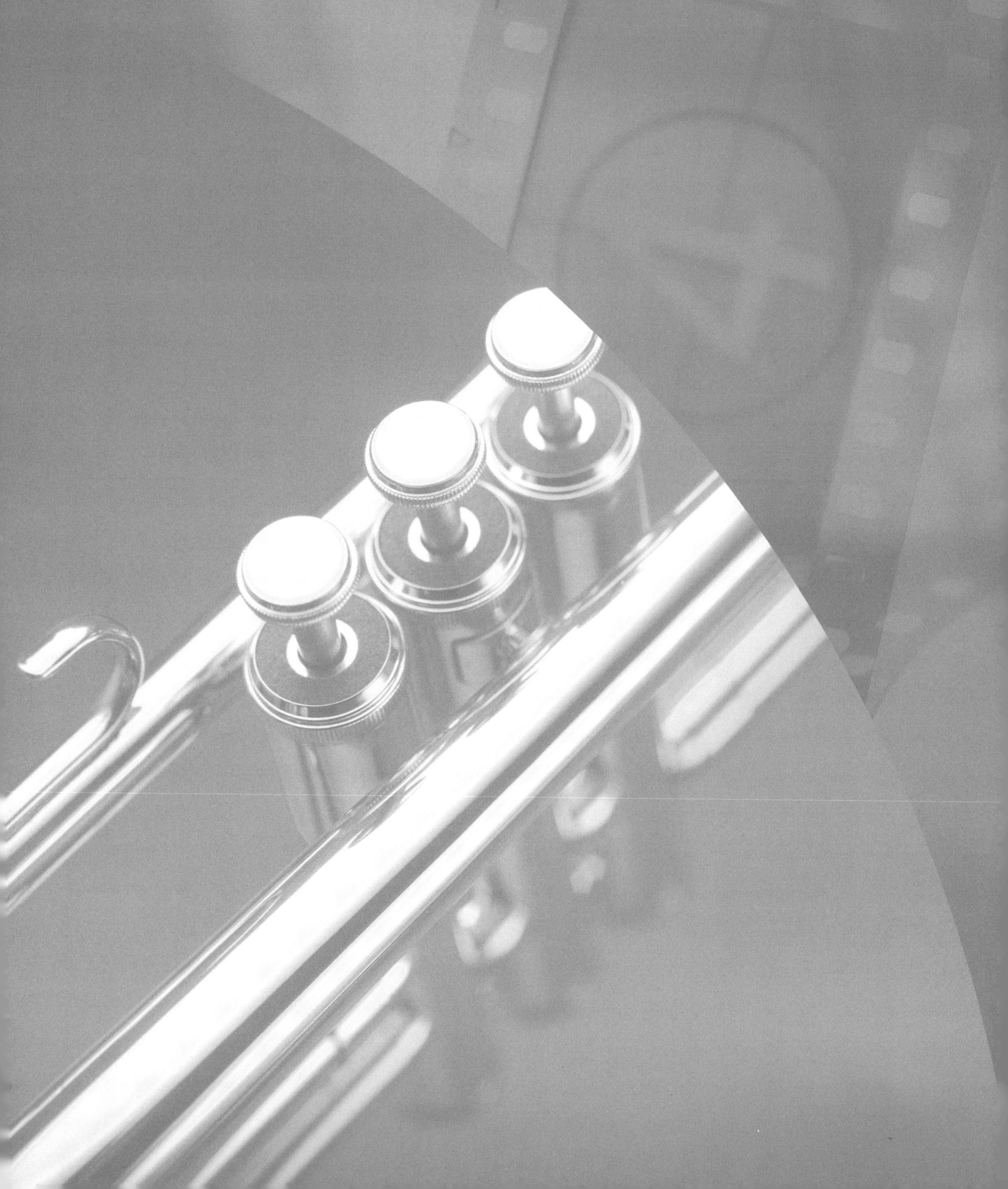

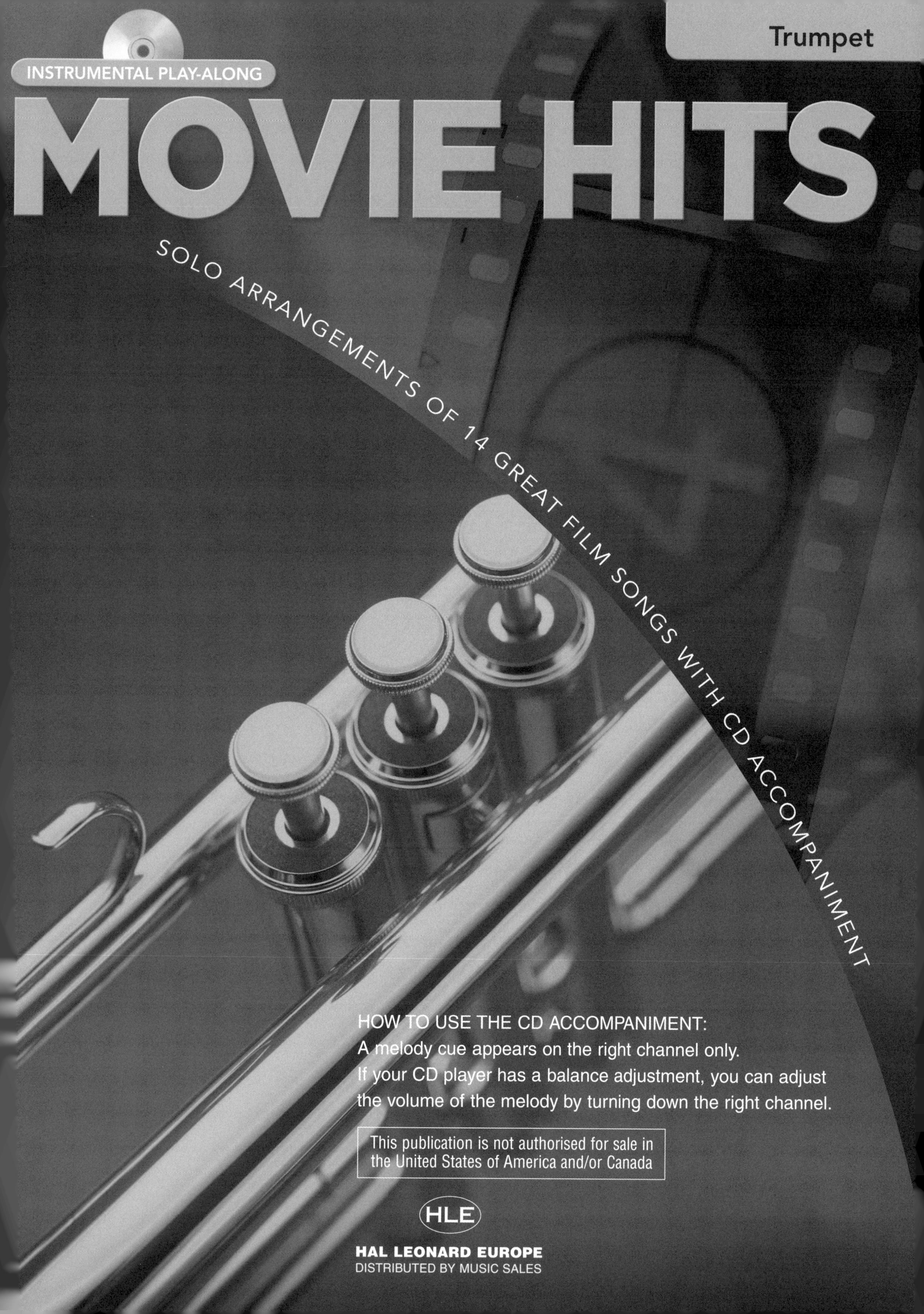

Trumpet

INSTRUMENTAL PLAY-ALONG

MOVIE HITS

SOLO ARRANGEMENTS OF 14 GREAT FILM SONGS WITH CD ACCOMPANIMENT

HOW TO USE THE CD ACCOMPANIMENT:
A melody cue appears on the right channel only.
If your CD player has a balance adjustment, you can adjust the volume of the melody by turning down the right channel.

HLE

HAL LEONARD EUROPE
DISTRIBUTED BY MUSIC SALES

Exclusive Distributors:
Music Sales Limited
14-15 Berners Street, London W1T 3LJ, UK.

Order No. HLE90002957
ISBN-13: 978-1-84609-379-1

Printed in the USA

Your Guarantee of Quality
As publishers, we strive to produce every book to the highest commercial standards. The book has been carefully designed to minimise awkward page turns and to make playing from it a real pleasure. Throughout, the printing and binding have been planned to ensure a sturdy, attractive publication which should give years of enjoyment. If your copy fails to meet our high standards, please inform us and we will gladly replace it.

www.musicsales.com

1 AN AMERICAN SYMPHONY

(Movement 3 Excerpts)

from MR. HOLLAND'S OPUS

TRUMPET

By MICHAEL KAMEN

❷ BACK TO THE FUTURE

from the Universal Motion Picture BACK TO THE FUTURE

TRUMPET

By ALAN SILVESTRI

BELIEVE

from Warner Bros. Pictures' THE POLAR EXPRESS

TRUMPET

Words and Music by GLEN BALLARD
and ALAN SILVESTRI

Moderately slow

5 THEME FROM E.T. THE EXTRA-TERRESTRIAL

from the Universal Picture E.T. THE EXTRA-TERRESTRIAL

TRUMPET

Music by
JOHN WILLIAMS

4 COME WHAT MAY

from the Motion Picture MOULIN ROUGE!

TRUMPET

Words and Music by
DAVID BAERWALD

mp
mf
D.S. al Coda
CODA
f
mp
f
rall.
mf

6 FORREST GUMP – MAIN TITLE

(Feather Theme)

TRUMPET

from the Paramount Motion Picture FORREST GUMP

Music by
ALAN SILVESTRI

7 THEME FROM 'JURASSIC PARK'

from the Universal Motion Picture JURASSIC PARK

TRUMPET

Composed by
JOHN WILLIAMS

8 LEARN TO BE LONELY

from THE PHANTOM OF THE OPERA

TRUMPET

Music by ANDREW LLOYD WEBBER
Lyrics by CHARLES HART

Moderato rubato

9 MISSION: IMPOSSIBLE THEME

from the Paramount Motion Picture MISSION: IMPOSSIBLE

TRUMPET

By LALO SCHIFRIN

◆10 MY HEART WILL GO ON

(Love Theme From 'Titanic')

From the Paramount and Twentieth Century Fox Motion Picture TITANIC

TRUMPET

Music by JAMES HORNER
Lyric by WILL JENNINGS

Irish Flute/Guitar
f
mp
rit.
p
Orch.

11 THEME FROM 'SCHINDLER'S LIST'

from the Universal Motion Picture SCHINDLER'S LIST

TRUMPET

Composed by JOHN WILLIAMS

12 THEME FROM SPIDER-MAN

from SPIDER-MAN

TRUMPET

Written by BOB HARRIS
and PAUL FRANCIS WEBSTER

13 STAR TREK® THE MOTION PICTURE

Theme from the Paramount Picture STAR TREK: THE MOTION PICTURE

TRUMPET

Music by
JERRY GOLDSMITH

14 YOU MUST LOVE ME

From the Cinergi Motion Picture EVITA

TRUMPET

Words by TIM RICE
Music by ANDREW LLOYD WEBBER